Trick-or-T

For Diabete

A Halloween Story For Kids Living With Diabetes

Published by
JayJo Books, LLC.
Publishing Special Books for Special Kids®
P.O. Box 213
Valley Park, MO 63088-0213

Edited by Laura Ditto
Designed & Illustrated by Tom Dineen

Library of Congress Cataloging-in-Publication Data
Gosselin, Kim
Trick-Or-Treat For Diabetes/Kim Gosselin - First Edition
Library of Congress Catalog Card Number 99-71577
1. Juvenile/Fiction/Children's Literature
2. Health Education
3. Diabetes
4. Children's Disabilities
ISBN 1-891383-07-8
Library of Congress

*All books printed by JayJo Books, LLC. are available at special quantity discounts when purchased in bulk. Special imprints, logos, messages and excerpts can be designed to meet your needs. For more information call the publisher at 636-861-1331 or fax at 636-861-2411. E-mail us at jayjobooks@aol.com.

JayJo Books, LLC.
Publishing Special Books for Special Kids®
P.O. Box 213
Valley Park, MO 63088-0213

A Note From The Author

This book was written for all children living with Type 1 Diabetes whose families and others sometimes don't realize that there are creative ways to allow these children to take part in this imaginative, traditional holiday we know as, Halloween. For the last seven years on October 31st, my son has taken turns dressing up as a "Sesame Street"® character, cowboy, clown, monster, pirate, ghost or goblin.

*It's important for all of us to realize that Halloween is much more than a holiday about candy. Halloween is a tradition inspiring creativity, fun, socialization and make-believe. Believe it or not, there are still those who think children living with diabetes can't **ever** eat candy, when indeed, sometimes candy or a sugary treat may save the child's life!*

More importantly, why take this magical social tradition away from children living with diabetes, when in fact, they are really no different from any other child? After all, our common goal as parents and caregivers is to give all of our children confidence and independence in all facets of the world around us. With a little common sense, creativity, proper medication and monitoring, kids with diabetes can be allowed to participate in the magic of Halloween just like all of their friends.

Happy Holidays,
Kim Gosselin

Sarah pricked her finger, carefully putting the blood on the test strip. Soon she would know how high her blood sugar was and when she should get her insulin shot. Sarah was starving! Sure enough, her blood sugar was below her normal range-72! "Normal" for Sarah was usually somewhere between 80 and 150.

Sarah carefully measured her insulin into the syringe while her mom kept a watchful eye. Even though diabetes was new to the whole family, they all seemed to be doing pretty well with it. Sarah knew what she had to do to stay in good control (like the diabetes doctors and nurses had explained to her) and she took it seriously. She gave herself her shot and quickly fixed her measured breakfast of cereal, toast, milk and orange juice.

Sarah's mother noticed that her daughter didn't seem her "old self" this morning. She acted kind of depressed and not very talkative.

"What's bothering you, Sarah?"

"Oh, not much, Mom," she answered, frowning. "The school is having a Halloween party today. It's my first party since I found out I have diabetes. I really don't even feel like going."

"You know, Sarah, you can still go and have a good time. Parties are special times and you can usually even have some of the 'treats' if you work them into your meal plan."

"You mean it, Mom? I thought having diabetes meant that I couldn't eat anything with sugar in it unless I was 'low'."

"Like I said, school parties are special days. I'll call the teacher and find out what they're planning. She can pass you a note to tell you what your best choices are, how's that? You can probably just exchange a starch for a plain cookie or something like that."

"Thanks, Mom," Sarah said, giving her mom a great big hug. "Everything always feels so much better when I talk to you about it."

"Yeah, and don't ever forget it," her mom answered, playfully patting her on the behind. "Now get off to school, before you miss the bus. I'll call your teacher."

Later that afternoon, the school Halloween party was great! Sarah had fun decorating pumpkin cookies (eating one without the frosting, and saving the other for a "low"). Sarah realized that having diabetes didn't stop her from playing the same games as all the other kids, either. If she got candy for a "prize", she simply put it in her backpack for a "low". Sometimes, she shared her treats with her best friends, too!

There was one thing that still bothered Sarah about Halloween. In a few days all of her friends would be having fun going "trick-or-treating". Sarah knew she couldn't eat candy very much any more. She knew how important it was to keep her blood sugar in good control. Would she have to miss "trick-or-treating" altogether?!

That afternoon, when Sarah jumped off the school bus, she ran home to tell her mother all about the Halloween party. She had so much fun that she couldn't wait to share it with her!

"Mom, you won't believe it! None of the kids *even* talked about my diabetes and I got to do everything they did! I even decorated pumpkin cookies!" she said as she excitedly showed her mother the one she brought home.

"Having diabetes doesn't mean you have to quit doing everything you did before! You still are a very lucky girl, Sarah. Did your teacher help you decide what to eat today?"

"Yeah, she was awesome," answered Sarah. "She passed me a note and told me to skip my starch exchange at snack time and to eat the unfrosted cookie instead of my crackers. I checked my blood sugar at school and everything worked out perfectly!"

"Good," answered Sarah's mother. "I talked to your teacher earlier this morning and that's exactly what I asked her to do. I'm glad it all worked out for you and that you had such a good time," she said, giving Sarah another big hug.

That night, Sarah tossed and turned in bed. No matter how hard she tried, she couldn't quite get to sleep. She kept thinking about "trick-or-treating". She wanted to go <u>so</u> <u>bad</u> with all of her friends, but what GOOD would it do? Sarah knew she could never eat THAT much candy! And, it wasn't good for her body to have a lot of "lows" either! Finally, as the bright yellow moon rose above the dark blue sky, silent sleep fell upon Sarah's half-closed eyes.

The next morning, as the sun peeked over the morning horizon, Sarah got up and dressed for school. She decided to talk to her mom about "trick-or-treating". First, of course, Sarah needed to check her blood sugar and give herself her morning shot before she ate breakfast.

During her meal, Sarah brought up the subject of
"trick-or-treating" with her mom at the breakfast table.

"Mom, do kids living with diabetes get to go 'trick-or-treating'? I
know I can't eat all the candy, but it would be fun to go out with
my friends."

"I'll think about it while you're at school today and come up with
an idea to talk about later," she said with a wink.

"Thanks, Mom. You're the BEST!"

All that morning and afternoon, Sarah's mom thought of how she could make "trick-or-treating" special for Sarah. She knew Sarah could save some of her candy for when she felt "low" (and needed to eat sugar, FAST!). Still, how could she keep Sarah from wanting *all* of it, especially when her friends were eating theirs whenever they wanted to?

There was no way Sarah could eat all the candy she would collect on Halloween night. The more Sarah's mom thought about it though, the more she remembered how she felt as a kid when she was Sarah's age. She remembered having lots of fun going "trick-or-treating"! And, it wasn't all about eating candy either!

After all, thought Sarah's mom, there was a lot more to Halloween than candy. It was about dressing up in funny costumes, being silly, sharing scary times with friends and just plain having fun! Just because Sarah had diabetes didn't mean EVERYTHING had to change!

Later that afternoon, Sarah's mom talked to Sarah's grandmother about what to do. Together, they came up with a great idea! The most important thing was for Sarah to be excited about going out "trick-or-treating" with all her friends!

Sarah's mom and grandmother were sure that they had come up with a way to do just that! Instead of Sarah having to think about all the candy she COULDN'T eat, they came up with the idea to "buy" her candy from her (for a small fee).

This meant Sarah could go out and buy herself something special without feeling left out. It would be a lot better for her not to eat candy anyway! And, she could still pick out a few of her very favorite treats for "lows". They would keep a small bag at home and take another one to the school nurse!

It wasn't long before Sarah was back home from school. Her mother couldn't wait to tell her of her plan! Sarah sat on the sofa and listened with a great big smile on her face. She thought her mother's idea was perfect! Because they were going to "buy" her candy, she was just as excited about going with her friends "trick-or-treating" as anyone else would be. This would be the best Halloween ever!!

A few nights later, Sarah came down the family staircase in her
newly bought witch's costume. Soon the doorbell rang. Sarah's
mom answered it only to find all of her daughter's friends waiting
for her. There were goblins and ghosts, princesses, queens,
dragons, and devils! All were waiting for Sarah to join in the fun!

"Bye, Mom," Sarah said running out the front door. "I've got my meter with me just in case I feel 'low'. Then I guess I could always eat some candy," she said with a smile across her face.

"Just be careful, and have lots of fun," Sarah's mother told her. "Try not to collect too much candy," she added, smiling.

"I don't want to go broke," she kidded!

Halloween night flew by as Sarah and her friends had the most fun they've ever had. Sarah felt "low", so she stopped to check her blood sugar while all of her friends waited for her. Since she *was* "low", she picked a favorite chocolate bar from her "pumpkin" of goodies and munched it down quickly.

Sarah came home from her evening of fun and dumped all of her candy on the floor of the kitchen for her and her mother to count. She made nearly $10.00 on her haul! Sarah then picked out her favorite candy for "lows" at home and made a separate bag to take to the school nurse.

That night, lying in bed, Sarah truly thought that having diabetes really wasn't all that bad. She realized life was simply what you made of it. If you really wanted to, you could still do almost anything! Even "trick-or-treating" on Halloween!

The End